British Library Cataloguing in Publication Data
A Catalogue record for this book is available from the British Library

ISBN 978 0 340 68325 5

10 9 8 7 6 5 4 3 2

First published 1997
by Hodder Children's Books
a division of Hachette Children's Books
338 Euston Road. London NW1 3BH

Printed in China

Albertine

Anna Currey

Hodder
Children's
Books

a division of Hodder Headline plc

To Robert
with love

Albertine decided not to
lay her eggs in the sand
like the other dinosaurs.
She wanted something
special for her eggs.

So Albertine and Hector built a house.

They built it out of banana leaves and giant horsetail

When the house was finished it was beautiful.
All their friends came to see how lovely it was.
"It's lovely!" they said. "What is it?"
"It's a house," explained Albertine.
"I'm going to live in it and lay eggs.
Come and look inside."

And they were just about to when...

...something awful happened.

A giant diplodocus lumbered along...

...and ate it for breakfast.

"Oh dear," said the diplodocus
as he swallowed the last mouthful.
"I'm frightfully sorry."

Albertine was most upset.

"Never mind dear," said Hector.
"We'll build you a new one."
"It won't take long," said her friends.

So Albertine sat and waited while they built her a new house.

They built it out of banana leaves

and giant horsetail

and tree-fern fronds.

When the house was finished,
it was absolutely beautiful,
and they were just going to show
Albertine what it looked like inside,

when Something Awful Happened.

"I just came back,"
said the diplodocus,
sitting down very heavily indeed,
"to say how really really really
sorry I am about eating your house,
and It Won't Occur Again."

So it was that dinosaurs never really
took to building houses after that

but carried on laying their eggs
in the sand as they always had done.